Walt Disney's

The Jungle Book

Adapted from the film by Jim Razzi

Disney
PRESS

New York

3 5 7 9 10 8 6 4 2

Library of Congress Catalog Card Number: 91-58975
ISBN: 1-56282-243-8

1

Many strange tales are told of the jungles in India, but none so strange as the story of a young boy named Mowgli, the Man-cub who was raised by wolves. . . .

It all began on the day Bagheera, the panther, heard an unfamiliar sound echo through the jungle. It was the sound of a baby crying.

Bagheera loped along the banks of the river until he came upon a half-sunken boat. There he found a baby boy lying in a basket.

"Why, it's a Man-cub," he said.

The big panther picked up the basket and placed it gently on the bank. He gazed curiously at the Man-cub, who by now had stopped crying and was staring back at Bagheera with big brown eyes.

Bagheera smiled down at the baby, and the baby suddenly smiled back in return.

"Hmm," Bagheera murmured. "I have saved you from the river, but what do I do with you now? You will have to have nourishment and a mother's care."

As Bagheera was musing on this, the Man-cub reached up and grabbed some of his stiff whiskers.

"No, no, little one," said Bagheera. "I have no time to play. I must think."

Then a thought occurred to the gentle panther. He knew there was a wolf family, living in a nearby cave, that had just been blessed with a litter of cubs.

"Perhaps if I take the Man-cub to the mother wolf," he said to himself, "she will take care of him."

He nodded at the baby as if he understood.

"Good, it's decided then," he said in his slightly stuffy manner. "I will take you there now."

So without wasting another moment, Bagheera picked up the basket and carried it to the cave.

He placed the basket in front of the entrance, where the wolves were sure to see it. Then he found a suitable hiding spot and waited.

But after a few minutes went by, Bagheera became impatient. The baby was silent now and no one was coming out of the cave.

The big panther crept over to the basket and gave it a swipe with his paw. The baby squalled in protest and Bagheera jumped back with startled eyes. What a healthy pair of lungs the Man-cub had!

But the idea worked, because as soon as Bagheera reached his hiding place again, a pack of cubs came scampering out of the cave and padded over to the basket.

The mother wolf followed her cubs out of the cave, and when she saw the baby, she smiled.

"Oh, a little Man-cub," she cried. "I have never seen one. Look how small he is and how unafraid. Why, he is as bold as one of my cubs!"

Bagheera smiled too when he heard that. "I just knew there wouldn't be a problem, thanks to the maternal instinct," the panther chuckled.

But then he saw Rama, the father, stalk out of the cave.

Bagheera wasn't so sure about Rama.

What if Rama doesn't accept the baby? he thought. What if he gets angry? What if . . .

But Rama was already approaching the basket as if it were a strange animal. And just when the big wolf stuck his nose in the basket, the baby laughed.

Bagheera held his breath.

But Rama only smiled.

The big panther let out a long sigh.

It was going to be all right now. The Man-cub had been accepted into the wolf family.

2

*T*en times the yearly rains had come, and the Man-cub had grown up as strong and sturdy as his wolf brothers and sisters.

The wolf mother had named him Mowgli, which means "little frog." That was because, like a little frog, he could never stay still.

All day long Mowgli would run and play with the rest of the cubs, as fleet and surefooted as any of them.

Mowgli loved his family. And no one else, neither man nor beast, was ever happier in the jungle.

But one day, news spread throughout Mowgli's part of the jungle that Shere Khan, the tiger, was back after a long absence.

The wolves had a meeting about it on Council Rock. Even Bagheera was there, sitting on the limb of a nearby tree.

Akela was the leader of the pack, and it was he who reminded the others of the terrible danger the tiger represented.

"When Shere Khan hears there is a Man-cub here," Akela said, "he will surely kill the boy and all who protect him."

The other wolves nodded their heads in agreement.

"Then it's settled," said Akela. "For the safety of the pack, the Man-cub must go."

There was another chorus of agreement, and then Akela spoke again.

"Now it is my unpleasant duty to inform the boy's father, Rama."

Rama had been sitting away from the pack by himself. But now Akela called to him.

"Rama, come over here, please."

"Yes, Akela," said Rama.

"The Man-cub can no longer stay with the pack."

Although Rama had been expecting something like this, he was still shocked.

"But . . . the Man-cub . . . why, he's like my own son."

Akela looked at Rama kindly and said, "Rama, you know even the strength of the pack is no match for the tiger."

Rama nodded his head slowly. He knew what Akela said was true.

He looked around with tear-filled eyes.

"But it's not fair. The boy cannot survive alone in the jungle," he protested.

At that moment Bagheera, who had been listening to all this from his perch in the tree, lightly stepped down.

"Perhaps I can be of help," he announced.

"You, Bagheera? How?" asked Akela.

"I know a Man-village where he'll be safe," answered Bagheera. "Mowgli and I have taken many walks in the jungle together, so I'm sure he'll go with me."

"So be it," agreed Akela. "And go quickly— now. There is no time to lose."

And so it was that later that night, Mowgli found himself astride Bagheera's back, wending through the deep dark jungle.

The ride had been fun, but now Mowgli was tired and ready to go home.

"Bagheera," he murmured as he stifled a yawn, "I'm getting a little sleepy. Shouldn't we start back home?"

"We're not going back," answered Bagheera.

"I'm taking you to the Man-village."

Mowgli opened his eyes wide.

"The Man-village! But why?" he asked.

"Because Shere Khan, the tiger, has returned to this part of the jungle," answered Bagheera. "And he has sworn to kill you."

"Kill me?" cried Mowgli. "But why would he want to do that?"

"He hates man," answered Bagheera. "And Shere Khan is not going to allow you to grow up to become a man—another hunter with a gun."

Mowgli shook his head innocently.

"Oh, well then," he said, jumping off Bagheera's back. "We'll just explain to him that I'd never do a thing like that."

Bagheera shook his own head slowly and looked at Mowgli as if the boy were a slow-witted monkey.

"Don't be foolish," he said. "No one explains anything to Shere Khan."

At that, Mowgli stuck out his chin and cried, "Well, I'm not afraid of Shere Khan or anybody!"

Just then they came to a big sprawling tree.

"Now that's enough," said Bagheera, eyeing the tree. "We'll spend the night here. And when tomorrow comes, things will look much better."

But Mowgli didn't think so. He didn't want to spend the night in the tree, and he certainly didn't want to go to the Man-village. He wanted to spend the night with his family, and he wanted to stay in the jungle.

"Man-cub!"

Bagheera's stern voice interrupted Mowgli's thoughts.

"Up, up in the tree, I said." Then in a kinder tone, Bagheera said, "Go on, go up. You'll be safer there."

Mowgli looked down and scuffed the ground with his toe.

"But I don't want to go to the Man-village!" he cried. "And I don't want to climb this tree!"

Then he looked up.

"And anyway, I can't go way up there," he protested.

But Bagheera wouldn't be put off. With prods and pushes, he forced Mowgli up into the tree.

When they got to a suitable limb, Bagheera yawned and settled down for the night. Mowgli sat glumly on the opposite end of the limb.

"I want to stay in the jungle," he said, half to himself. "I can look after myself if I have to."

But Bagheera had hardly heard a word. He was

already half-asleep.

Just then Kaa, the python, who had been coiled around the upper branches of the tree, spied the little boy seated on the limb.

The long snake slowly uncoiled himself and smiled.

"Sssay now, what have we here?" he hissed. "Why, it's a Man-cub. A delicious Man-cub."

And with that he licked his fangs and slithered down from his perch.

3

When Kaa slithered over to Mowgli he expected the little boy to jump in fright. Instead, Mowgli took one look and said, "Oh, go away and leave me alone!"

But Kaa wasn't to be put off that easily. He knew he had a snaky charm that could lull even the most excitable beast into a dreamy trance. So he started to sway in front of Mowgli and speak in a soft, whispery voice. And in spite of himself, Mowgli started to feel drowsy.

"Yesss, Man-cub," whispered Kaa. "You *are* tired. Go to sssleep. Please go to sssleep."

And as Kaa was speaking in this seductive manner, he coiled his tail behind Mowgli.

Mowgli felt his eyes grow heavy as he watched the swaying snake. He tried very hard to stay awake, but his head felt as heavy as a beehive full of honey.

Then, as the little boy sat there helplessly, Kaa's tail coiled itself around Mowgli's entire body and started to squeeze tight.

Mowgli managed to turn his head toward Bagheera.

"Ah, Bah . . . Bah . . . Bagheera. Help!" he cried.

But Bagheera had his eyes closed and thought that Mowgli was still complaining.

"Oh, no, no. Look, there's no use arguing anymore. Now go to sleep and no more talk till morning."

By now the python had Mowgli completely in his grip, and as Bagheera finished speaking Kaa laughed and said, "Ha, ha, he won't be here in the morning!"

At that, Bagheera's eyes flew open and he jerked his head around. Without thinking twice, Bagheera pounced forward and swiped Kaa in the head with his big paw.

Kaa's head banged against the tree limb, and the long snake started to unwind from around Mowgli like a limp rubber band.

"Ughh," Kaa moaned as he forgot all about Mowgli and started toward Bagheera along the limb. "You have made a very ssserious and ssstupid missstake, my friend."

Although Bagheera was brave enough, he knew Kaa's powers. He worried that he had acted too hastily. Still, he couldn't let any harm come to Mowgli, no matter what the cost.

As Kaa came closer he repeated, "A ssstupid missstake . . ."

"Now, now, now, Kaa, I was . . . ," Bagheera started to say as he frantically swiveled his head from side to side, looking for a chance to escape.

"Look me in the eyes when I'm speaking to you!" Kaa ordered. "Both eyes!"

Bagheera was getting tired of moving his head, and Kaa was right in front of him. He had no choice but to do as he was told.

Kaa was so busy hypnotizing Bagheera, he forgot all about Mowgli, who was slowly pushing the snake's long, coiled tail off the limb.

Just as Kaa was about to entwine Bagheera, the weight of his own tail whipped him off the limb. He went slithering and sliding down the tree, banging his head against the trunk along the way.

Kaa finally landed in a heap on the ground with a knot in his tail and a lump on his head.

Moaning and groaning, the long snake awkwardly slithered into the bushes and disappeared from sight.

Mowgli laughed and then went over to Bagheera.

"I did it!" he cried. "I saved us!"

But Bagheera, still in a trance, looked at him with glazed eyes.

"Wake up, Bagheera, wake up!" Mowgli shouted.

"Ah. . . . Ah, what happened?" Bagheera finally asked.

"Kaa hypnotized you and I saved us!" Mowgli said. "If it wasn't for me, you wouldn't be here."

Bagheera tried to regain as much of his dignity as he could.

"Harumph!" he sniffed. "Yes, but if it wasn't for *me, you* wouldn't be here to tell me I wouldn't be here."

Then Bagheera looked up at the star-studded sky.

"Let's rest now," he said. "We have a long journey ahead of us tomorrow."

A few hours later, as the sun peeked over the horizon, Mowgli stirred and sleepily blinked his eyes open. Bagheera was still asleep, and Mowgli was about to wake him when he heard a big commotion. It sounded like a thousand animals were tramping through the jungle. Even the ground underneath their tree shook with the vibrations.

"Wake up, Bagheera, wake up!" Mowgli cried. "Something's coming!"

Suddenly he heard a gruff voice shouting, "Hup, two, three, four. Keep it up, two, three, four!"

Mowgli crawled along the limb and peered into the tangled forest. There was nothing to be seen—yet.

He crawled back to Bagheera—whatever was coming might be dangerous.

4

As Mowgli shook Bagheera awake, a herd of elephants suddenly appeared, marching in single file through the jungle.

"It's a parade!" Mowgli shouted in relief.

Bagheera put his paws over his ears and groaned, "Oh no, it's Colonel Hathi's Dawn Patrol again!"

"What's the Dawn Patrol?" asked Mowgli as he grabbed a vine and slid to the ground.

"Every day at dawn, Colonel Hathi drills his herd in military maneuvers," Bagheera answered. "I usually try to be somewhere else at the time."

Mowgli laughed and ran to get a closer look at the marching elephants.

As Mowgli approached the herd, he fell into step beside a baby elephant.

"Hello," he said. "What are you doing?"

"Shhh," answered the baby elephant. "Drilling."

"Can I do it too?" asked Mowgli.

"Sure," answered the baby elephant. "Just do what I do. But don't talk in ranks. It's against regulations."

Mowgli got down on all fours and started to march along with the baby elephant. From way up front, he could hear Colonel Hathi shouting, "Hup, two, three, four! Keep it up, two, three, four!"

Mowgli was about to ask another question when Colonel Hathi shouted, "Ho! Company, halt!"

The baby elephant turned to Mowgli and said, "That means stop."

Mowgli nodded and stopped marching along with the rest of the herd.

Colonel Hathi then started to come down the line as the elephants stood in a row, ear to ear.

A big elephant named Winifred sighed and said, "March, march, march. My feet are killing me."

The baby elephant smiled and said, "That's my mom."

Mowgli's eyes widened.

"Your mom marches too?" he said.

"Yep," answered the baby elephant. "So does my pop."

"Who's your pop?" asked Mowgli.

The baby elephant raised his little trunk and

pointed to Colonel Hathi.

"Ohh," said Mowgli, "I . . ."

Suddenly he heard the colonel shout, "Silence in the ranks!"

Mowgli stood stock-still as the colonel marched up and down the line behind him.

"Dress up that line!" commanded the colonel. "Pull in those tails!"

Then the colonel came around to the front.

"Inspection!" he cried.

All the elephants quickly raised their trunks.

"Psst," whispered the baby elephant to Mowgli. "Stick your nose up."

Mowgli stuck his nose in the air as high as it could go.

"Like this?" he asked.

"Perfect," answered the baby elephant.

Colonel Hathi moved slowly down the line, inspecting each elephant along the way.

"Let's have a little more spit and polish on those bayonets!" he said as he peered at one elephant's dirty tusks.

"Esprit de corps," he shouted. "That's how I earned my commission in the maharaja's Fifth Pachyderm Brigade."

"What's pac-a-derm?" asked Mowgli.

"An elephant," answered the baby.

Suddenly Mowgli had an itch behind his left ear. He was just about to scratch it when he saw Colonel Hathi approach. He quickly stifled the urge and stood at attention.

Colonel Hathi stopped in front of the baby elephant and smiled.

"Keep those heels together, shall we, Son?"

"Okay, Pop, er, I mean . . . sir," the baby answered.

Colonel Hathi nodded and then stood in front of Mowgli.

"Ah, a new recruit," he said.

Colonel Hathi smiled for a moment, but then he tapped Mowgli rather hard on the nose and said, "I say, what happened to your trunk?"

Mowgli looked up and cried, "Hey, that hurts!"

Colonel Hathi knit his eyebrows together in an angry frown and he picked up Mowgli in his trunk.

"What's this?" he cried. "A Man-cub! Oh, this is treason! I'll have no Man-cub in my jungle!"

Then he plopped Mowgli down next to the baby elephant and glowered at him.

Before Mowgli could figure out what was going to happen next, Bagheera bounded up beside the colonel.

"I can explain, Hathi," Bagheera said.

"*Colonel* Hathi if you please, sir," answered the elephant.

"Oh yes, yes, Colonel Hathi," Bagheera went on. "Eh, ah, the Man-cub is with me. I'm taking him to the Man-village."

"To stay?" asked the colonel with a suspicious look.

Bagheera nodded.

"You have the word of Bagheera," he said.

"Good," said the colonel. "And remember, an elephant never forgets."

At that, the colonel gave the order to move out and the Dawn Patrol went on its way, stumbling and bumbling through the jungle.

Mowgli laughed and said, "That was fun!"

But Bagheera looked at him sternly and said, "It might have seemed fun to you, but when an elephant gets mad, it's not funny."

He looked around at the thick jungle.

"Now let's be on our way before anything else happens."

"Bagheera, where are we going?" Mowgli asked.

"You're going to the Man-village right now," Bagheera replied.

"I am not!" Mowgli snapped.

"Oh, yes you are," said Bagheera.

Mowgli shook his head and grabbed on to a nearby sapling. He hugged the tree and stuck out his chin.

"I'm staying right here!" he shouted.

"You're going to the Man-village if I have to drag you there every step of the way!" Bagheera said as he grabbed Mowgli by the britches.

"You let go of me!" Mowgli yelled.

Bagheera pulled, but Mowgli held on to the tree. Bagheera pulled again—this time a little harder. Mowgli still clung stubbornly to the tree.

Now Bagheera gave a mighty yank, but as he did so, he suddenly lost his grip. He flew backward as if he had been shot from a slingshot and landed with a loud splash in a large pond. He slunk out of the water, dripping wet and as mad as a drenched cat could be.

"That does it!" he cried. "From now on, you're on your own—alone!"

"Don't worry about me," answered Mowgli.

"I won't!" huffed Bagheera. And with that, he turned and made his way through the jungle brush and disappeared from sight.

Mowgli turned away and, after walking a bit, finally sat down with his back against a large rock.

"I can take care of myself," he said aloud. "I don't need anybody to look after me."

But as he sat there, surrounded by the deep, green jungle, he began to feel just a *little* worried.

5

Mowgli's thoughts were soon interrupted by the sound of a very loud and cheerful voice—someone was singing! He looked up just in time to see Baloo the bear shuffling out of the jungle brush.

"Well, now, ha ha. What have we here?" Baloo chuckled as he spied Mowgli.

The big bear sauntered over and sniffed Mowgli with his long wet nose.

Mowgli reached up and slapped the bear on the nose. He was in no mood to be bothered.

"Ouch!" Baloo cried. "Hey, what's the matter? I'm just trying to be friendly."

"Go away and leave me alone," Mowgli muttered.

But Baloo wasn't bothered by a little slap. Like all bears, he liked to play rough-and-tumble games.

So he sat down beside Mowgli and patted him on the back.

"Well now, that's pretty big talk, little britches," he said.

"I'm big enough," cried Mowgli. He rose and hit Baloo in the stomach.

Baloo just laughed and shook his head.

"Tsk, tsk, pitiful," he said. "That punch hardly dented my fur."

Baloo picked Mowgli up in his big bear paws and then set him down again.

"Hey, kid, you need help, and old Baloo's gonna learn you to fight like a bear."

Baloo suddenly jumped up and danced around like a boxer, bobbing and weaving.

"All right now, kid, loosen up," he puffed.

At first Mowgli didn't react. But Baloo's antics were starting to amuse him. He finally jumped up and began circling around Baloo, imitating his movements.

"That's it," cried Baloo. "Now gimme a big bear growl. Scare me."

Mowgli bared his teeth and growled softly.

"No, no, no," said Baloo. "I'm talking about—GROWL!!!—like a big bear!"

Baloo's growl was so powerful that Mowgli was

blown backward by the force.

Mowgli regained his footing and growled back, this time with gusto.

"That's it!" cried Baloo. "You've got it now." And he growled back at Mowgli.

Then Mowgli growled back at Baloo.

They were making so much noise that the sound carried a long way through the jungle. It carried all the way to Bagheera, who by now was well on his way home.

The big panther pricked up his ears in alarm.

"The Man-cub's in trouble," he said to himself. "I . . . I shouldn't have left him alone."

With that, he spun around and leaped from tree to tree, rushing to Mowgli's aid.

But when Bagheera reached the spot where Mowgli and Baloo were playfully sparring, he collapsed in disgust.

"Oh, no," he groaned. "It's that shiftless, stupid jungle bum Baloo!"

But Mowgli and Baloo were having so much fun that they hardly noticed Bagheera.

"That's it, kid, weave around," Baloo cried as he bobbed and weaved himself.

"Look for an opening," he continued. "Now you're getting it."

Mowgli grinned and pushed a shock of hair out of his eyes. Then he tried to hit Baloo. But Baloo swiped him with a big paw and flipped Mowgli on his back.

"Oh, ha," sneered Bagheera. "Fine teacher you are, old iron claws. How do you expect your pupils to remember the lesson after you knock them senseless?"

Baloo looked to where Mowgli was shakily sitting up.

"Well, I . . . I didn't mean to lay it on him so hard. I . . ."

But Mowgli was already getting to his feet. With a purposeful look at Bagheera, he said, "I'm all right. I'm not hurt. I'm a lot tougher than *some* people think."

Baloo grinned back.

"You better believe it," he said.

Then Baloo cried, "Now, let's go once more. I want you to keep circling around or I'm gonna knock your roof in again."

Mowgli danced in close to Baloo and then, with a sudden movement, hit the bear right on the nose.

"Ohh," Baloo cried. "Right on the button!"

Then he staggered back and fell in a heap on the ground. Mowgli scampered onto Baloo's belly and started to tickle him. Baloo squirmed and laughed.

"No, no, now, now. We don't do that here in the jungle. No tickling. I can't stand that tickling."

"Give up, Baloo?" Mowgli cried.

"Yes, ha, ha," Baloo cried back. "I give up."

When Mowgli had finally stopped tickling him, Baloo sat up and rubbed his chin with his paw.

"You're all right, kid," he said. "What do they call you?"

"Mowgli," answered Bagheera for him. "And he's going to the Man-village right now."

"Man-village?" Baloo looked shocked.

"Why, they'll ruin him. They'll make a man out of him."

Mowgli looked at Baloo and said, "Oh, Baloo. I want to stay here with you."

"Sure you do," answered Baloo.

"Oh?" Bagheera said. "And just how do you think he'll survive?"

"What do you mean?" answered Baloo. "He's with me, ain't he? And I'll learn him all I know."

"Well, that shouldn't take long," said Bagheera.

The remark went right over Baloo's head, and he nodded in agreement.

"You bet," he answered, tousling Mowgli's hair.

"It's like this, kid," he said. "All you've gotta do is look for the bare necessities."

"The *bear* necessities?" Mowgli repeated.

"Yes, the *bare* necessities," Baloo replied, suddenly breaking into a song about the simple needs of a bear in the jungle.

Bagheera could only look on helplessly as Baloo and Mowgli danced around eating bananas and coconuts. Mowgli was under Baloo's spell now. And he would never be convinced that the Man-village was the best place for him.

As Baloo continued singing, he jumped into the river and floated on his back. With a cry of glee, Mowgli hopped onto the bear's stomach and snuggled close.

The two of them floated lazily down the winding river as Bagheera watched from his perch on an overhanging limb.

"Oh, I give up," Bagheera sighed. "Well, I hope his luck holds out."

As Mowgli and Baloo floated farther away from Bagheera, he could hear Baloo say, "That's right, kid, all we need is the bare necessities. Why, I'll make a bear out of you yet."

Bagheera watched until they drifted out of sight. Then he slowly turned away.

6

"I like being a bear," Mowgli said as he and Baloo floated peacefully along. But even as Mowgli was speaking, a band of mischievous monkeys was following their journey down the river.

The monkeys were swinging among the tree branches that hung along the riverbank. As Mowgli and Baloo neared a low-hanging tree, one big monkey suddenly swooped down and snatched Mowgli off Baloo's stomach. A split second later, another monkey took Mowgli's place!

All this happened so fast that Mowgli didn't even have a chance to cry out.

For a moment, Baloo floated on, unaware. His eyes were closed and he had a dreamy expression on his face.

Just then a fly buzzed onto his nose.

"Hey, Mowgli," he drawled. "How about flicking that old mean fly off of your papa bear's nose?"

The monkey grinned and swatted Baloo's nose with a stick.

"Ouch!" Baloo cried, opening his eyes.

When he saw the monkey, he yelled in surprise and took a swipe at it.

"Why you flat-nosed, little-eyed, flaky creep!" he roared. "I'll murderlize ya!"

The monkey only laughed and scampered away.

Just as Baloo was about to go after it, he heard Mowgli cry, "Let go of me!"

Baloo looked up and saw another monkey holding Mowgli upside down by his feet.

"Take your flea-pickin' hands off my cub!" he shouted.

Baloo tried to stand in the water, but he stepped into a deep hole and dropped out of sight.

"That'll cool off a big hothead like him!" one of the monkeys snickered.

Baloo sputtered to the surface. And when he saw the monkeys carrying off Mowgli, he stumbled out of the river and shouted, "Give me back my Man-cub!"

But the monkeys just laughed and swung from tree to tree, carrying Mowgli along with them.

A few of them swung down close to Baloo and teased him. Baloo took one swipe after another—

A family of wolves finds an abandoned baby Man-cub. They take him in and name him Mowgli.

The leaders of the wolfpack believe that Mowgli is in danger from the tiger, Shere Khan, and must be sent to the Man-village.

The wise and gentle panther Bagheera dozes with Mowgli on a tree limb during their journey to the Man-village.

Kaa, a crafty snake, tries to hypnotize Mowgli.

Mowgli meets an army of elephants: Colonel Hathi and the Dawn Patrol.

Mowgli tries to join in but finds that marching is tricky!

After venturing out on his own, Mowgli meets a new friend, Baloo the bear, who tells him about "the bare necessities" of life.

Some mischievous monkeys grab Mowgli away from Baloo and take him off to see their king.

King Louie tells Mowgli, "I want to be human, like you!"

Disguised as a female monkey, Baloo sidles up to King Louie, hoping he can rescue the Man-cub.

Mowgli's not afraid of the slithery snake Kaa.

Shere Khan is looking for Mowgli, and Kaa lies to him, saying he hasn't seen the Man-cub.

A foursome of silly vultures vow to be Mowgli's friend.

When they finally meet, Mowgli tells Shere Khan, "I'm not afraid of you!"

Baloo's got the tiger by the tail—he tries to keep Shere Khan away from Mowgli.

A creature he has never seen before captures Mowgli's eye—a girl! Suddenly, the Man-village doesn't seem such a bad place after all.

mostly at empty air.

Then one of the monkeys threw a breadfruit at Baloo and hit him squarely on the head. Baloo fell flat on his back.

"There's some bear necessities!" laughed the monkey.

Baloo was wiping the juice of the fruit from his face when he heard Mowgli cry, "Baloo! Help me! They're carrying me away!"

The bear just lay stunned for a moment, not knowing what to do.

Then Baloo shouted, "Help, Bagheera, help!"

From up the river Bagheera heard the cry and sighed.

"Well, it's happened. They're in trouble," he said. "It took a little longer than I thought, but it's happened."

And with that, he raced to the rescue.

When Bagheera reached Baloo, however, there was no sign of Mowgli.

"All right," Bagheera said. "What happened? Where's Mowgli?"

"They ambushed me," Baloo answered indignantly. "Thousands of them. I jabbed with my left, and then I swung with my right, and then . . ."

"Oh, for the last time, what happened to

Mowgli?'' interrupted Bagheera.

"Like I told you,'' answered Baloo. "Those mangy monkeys carried him off.''

"They're taking him to their headquarters, the ancient ruins!'' cried Bagheera.

He shook his head in dismay.

"Oh, I hate to think of what will happen when he meets that king of theirs!''

7

Even as Bagheera was speaking, the monkeys were racing through the forest with their captive.

They didn't stop until they came to an enormous templelike ruin deep in the jungle.

And there, seated on a stone throne, was the monkey king himself!

The king smiled when he saw Mowgli.

"So you're the Man-cub," he said.

"Put me down!" yelled Mowgli.

The monkey holding Mowgli grinned and let go. The little boy fell in a sprawl at the king's feet.

Mowgli scrambled to his feet and glowered.

But the king just laughed and said, "Cool it boy. Unwind yourself."

"What do you want me for?" asked Mowgli.

Instead of answering right away, the monkey

king shot a banana out of its skin and straight into Mowgli's mouth.

"Let's be friends, chum," he said. "Word has grabbed my royal ear that you want to stay in the jungle."

Mowgli calmed down a bit.

"I sure do," he said.

"Mmm, that's good," answered the king. "And old King Louie—that's me—can fix it for you. Have we got a deal?"

"Yes, sir," answered Mowgli. "I'll do anything to stay in the jungle."

"Good," smiled King Louie. "Now I'll tell you what I want." And to Mowgli's surprise, King Louie suddenly went into a song and dance.

Mowgli looked on in amazement as the king explained—in between clapping and finger snapping—that what he wanted was to be human himself!

"You're doing pretty good so far," said Mowgli.

In spite of himself, Mowgli was soon singing and dancing along with the rest of the monkeys.

"Ha, ha," laughed Mowgli. "This is fun."

"Yeah, ain't it?" said King Louie. But as he continued to dance, he added, "Now all I need from you, little Man-cub, is the secret of man's red fire."

Mowgli gave King Louie a puzzled look. "But I don't know how to make fire," he explained.

"And anyway," he continued, "what's fire got to do with anything?"

King Louie tried to keep up his song but he frowned a little this time and said, "Don't try to trick me, Man-cub. I can't be a man without knowing how to make a fire."

While all this activity was going on, Baloo and Bagheera had finally reached the ancient ruins themselves and were now hidden from sight on top of a crumbling balcony. They listened carefully to King Louie's song.

"Man's red fire!" gasped Bagheera. "So that's what this is all about." He turned to Baloo and whispered, "We'd better move quickly."

"Yeah, let me at 'em. I'll tear that old king from limb to limb. I'll . . ."

"Stop that," answered Bagheera. "This will take brains, not brawn. Now here's what we'll do. You create a disturbance and I'll rescue Mowgli."

"What should I do?" asked Baloo.

"I told you—create a disturbance."

"Oh yeah, right," answered Baloo.

A few minutes later, a big female monkey sidled right up to King Louie and started dancing.

It was Baloo in disguise!

"Hey, where did you come from, beautiful?" asked King Louie.

Baloo just batted his eyelashes and chattered prettily.

King Louie was so taken by the big female that he didn't notice Bagheera creeping along the rubble of the old ruins, trying to get near Mowgli.

But as the dancing and singing became more frenzied, Baloo's disguise suddenly slipped off and the monkeys yelled, "It's Baloo the bear! How'd he get here?"

Mowgli, too, saw Baloo. And with a cry of joy, he ran up and jumped into his arms. At that, the monkeys started to chatter angrily, jumping and hopping all over the old ruins.

A real tug-and-shove fight began. One minute Baloo had Mowgli, and the next minute King Louie snatched Mowgli away. But, finally, Baloo grabbed Mowgli firmly and headed toward Bagheera.

As King Louie reached out to catch Baloo with his long arm, he accidentally knocked down one of the columns. The already crumbling ruins began to rumble and shake. . . .

When Baloo saw that Mowgli was safely on Bagheera's back, he turned around. King Louie was desperately trying to hold up the ancient walls himself. But it was no use. Baloo took a final swipe, and with a mighty roar, the ancient ruins came tumbling down on the monkeys, scattering them in all directions.

The battle was over.

8

*L*ater that night, Baloo, Bagheera, and Mowgli rested on a small island in the middle of a river.

Mowgli was fast asleep on a bed of soft leaves, but Bagheera was still lecturing Baloo.

"Mowgli seems to have man's ability to get into trouble," he said. "And your influence hasn't been exactly helpful."

Baloo looked over at Mowgli and replied, "Shhh. Keep it down. You're gonna wake up my little buddy. He's had a big day, you know," continued Baloo. "It ain't easy learnin' to be like me."

"Pah!" sniffed Bagheera. "A disgraceful performance. The way Mowgli cavorted with those scatterbrained apes."

"Aw, he was just monkeying around with them," answered Baloo.

Then the bear went over to the sleeping boy and gazed at him fondly.

"Baloo," whispered Bagheera. "I'd like a word with you."

Baloo nodded and shambled back to Bagheera.

"What's up, Baggy?" he asked.

Bagheera winced at the nickname but went on anyway.

"The Man-cub must go to the Man-village," he said. "The jungle is not the place for him."

"What's wrong with the jungle?" asked Baloo. "Take a look at me. *I* grew up in the jungle."

"Yes, and just look at yourself. You're a disreputable sight."

Baloo looked at his own reflection in the water and saw that he had a black eye and assorted bumps and bruises from the fight with the monkeys.

"Well, you don't look so good yourself," he said when he looked back at Bagheera.

Bagheera looked at his own reflection and saw that he, too, had a black eye.

"Oh, stop evading the issue," he sputtered. "The fact is that you can't adopt Mowgli as your son. He belongs in the Man-village. Birds of a feather should flock together."

Baloo smiled at Bagheera and said, "Stop worrying, Baggy, I'll take care of him."

"Yes," answered Bagheera. "Like you did when

the monkeys kidnapped him."

"So, can't a guy make one mistake?" retorted Baloo.

"Not in the jungle," said Bagheera. "And another thing. Sooner or later, Mowgli will meet Shere Khan."

"The tiger?" said Baloo. "What's he got against the kid?"

Bagheera had a serious look on his face as he moved closer to Baloo.

"He hates man with a vengeance," Bagheera explained. "And he fears man's gun and man's fire."

"But little Mowgli doesn't have those things," said Baloo.

"And Shere Khan won't wait until he does," said Bagheera. "He'll get Mowgli while he's still young and helpless."

Baloo looked dejected. He knew that what Bagheera said was true. He sat down on the ground and said, "Well, what am I gonna do then?"

"You will take Mowgli to the Man-village."

"But . . . but I promised the kid he could stay with me here in the jungle."

"That's just the point," said Bagheera. "As long as he's with you, he's in danger."

Baloo knew that Bagheera was right again. There was just one thing to do, and that was to take Mowgli to the Man-village. Baloo wiped a tear from his eye and looked up at the sky. It was getting light.

"It's morning now, Baloo," said Bagheera. "I think you and Mowgli should go right away."

Baloo sighed, padded over to the sleeping boy, and gently shook him awake.

9

A short while later Baloo and Mowgli were deep in the jungle, heading for the Man-village.

Mowgli was happily skipping along beside Baloo. "Where are we going?" he asked.

Baloo hadn't told Mowgli yet that he was taking him to the Man-village. He didn't know quite what to answer.

"Mowgli, ah, look, little buddy . . . ," he started. "There's somethin' I have to tell ya."

"What's that, Baloo?" asked Mowgli.

"I have to take you to the Man-village," Baloo finally blurted.

At that, tears filled Mowgli's eyes.

"The Man-village!" he cried. "But . . . but . . . you said we were partners. You said I could stay with you."

"Now look, kid, I, I can explain," stammered Baloo.

But Mowgli didn't wait to hear anything more. With one swift movement, he turned and ran into the jungle.

"Wait!" yelled Baloo. "Listen to old Baloo."

But Mowgli had already disappeared into the tangled forest.

Baloo raced after him desperately, but try as he might, he couldn't find a trace of the little boy.

"Mowgli!" he yelled. "Mowgli!"

At that moment Bagheera, who hadn't been far away, came bounding up to Baloo.

"Now what's happened?" he asked.

"The kid ran out on me," answered Baloo.

"Well, don't just stand there," cried Bagheera. "Let's separate. We've got to find him. Before . . ."

"Before what?" asked Baloo.

"Before Shere Khan does!" cried Bagheera.

At that very moment, and not very far away, Shere Khan himself was stalking a deer through the jungle.

The ferocious tiger was just about to spring on the unsuspecting creature when a loud noise distracted both him and the deer.

It was Colonel Hathi and his Dawn Patrol!

With a swish of its tail, the deer bounded away.

"What beastly luck!" snarled Shere Khan. "Confound that ridiculous Colonel Hathi."

Nevertheless, Shere Khan wanted no trouble with the elephants, so he crouched low in the bushes. He watched as the elephants tramped a short distance, and then he saw Bagheera come into view.

"Wait a minute. Halt!" Bagheera cried at the top of his lungs.

The elephants stopped so suddenly that they bumped into one another.

Without wasting a moment, Bagheera told Colonel Hathi about Mowgli and asked for his help in finding him.

"Absolutely impossible," roared Hathi. "We're on a cross-country march!"

"But it's an emergency, Colonel," cried Bagheera. "The Man-cub must be found before Shere Khan finds him."

"Nonsense, old boy," replied Colonel Hathi. "Shere Khan isn't within miles of here."

Bagheera was about to plead some more when Winifred stepped up to Colonel Hathi and said, "Just a minute, you pompous old windbag. How would you like it if our boy was lost—alone in the jungle?"

"Why, I . . . ," Colonel Hathi sputtered.

"Now you help find him, or I'm taking over command!"

At that remark Colonel Hathi's trunk bristled.

"All right," he finally said to Bagheera. "The Dawn Patrol will search for the lost boy."

Shere Khan had been listening to all this from his hiding place in the bushes. And now that he had heard it all, he rumbled deep in his chest.

"A lost Man-cub, alone in the jungle," he purred. "How interesting. I should do them all a good deed and find him first."

And with that he slunk away and headed into the bush.

10

At that same moment, not very far away, Mowgli had just sat down under a tree when Kaa's tail came down from the branches and scooped him up, pulling him into the tree.

When they were eye to eye, Kaa smiled.

"Well Man-cub, it's ssso nice to sssssee you again," he said as he placed Mowgli on a high limb.

But Mowgli didn't want anything to do with the crafty snake or anybody else for that matter.

"Go away and leave me alone," he cried as he untangled himself from Kaa's tail and looked away.

"You don't want to look at me, then?" asked Kaa as he tried, once again, to hypnotize Mowgli.

"No sir!" replied Mowgli. "I know what you're trying to do."

"Why, you have me all wrong," said Kaa innocently. "I just want to see to it that you never leave this jungle."

At that remark Mowgli softened a bit.

"How can you do that?" he asked.

"Oh, I have my own little ways," answered Kaa. "But first you must trust me."

Mowgli's brows went down.

"I don't trust anyone anymore," he said.

"I don't blame you," Kaa answered. "But surely you can trust *me*."

Mowgli wanted to believe Kaa. He wanted to believe anyone who could help him stay in the jungle. So he looked at Kaa and asked, "What can *you* do?"

"Why, now, I have to think about that," said Kaa. "Let me sleep on it."

Then he gazed at Mowgli with his big eyes.

"Why don't you sleep on it, too," he whispered.

Mowgli felt himself grow drowsy. Almost immediately, his eyes closed and he slumped down into Kaa's coils.

"That's it, sssleep," murmured Kaa. "Trust in me and sleep . . . ," hissed Kaa as he covered Mowgli completely in his coils.

Suddenly, Kaa felt someone pull on his tail from below. He slithered his head down and saw that it was Shere Khan.

"I'd like a word with you if you don't mind," purred Shere Khan. "I thought perhaps you were entertaining someone up there in your coils," he said. "I could swear I heard you talking to someone. Who is it, Kaa?" he asked as his giant paw wrapped around Kaa's throat.

"Who, me?" answered Kaa. "Who would I be talking to?"

"I've no time for this nonsense, Kaa. I'm busy searching for the lost Man-cub . . . ," purred the tiger.

"Man-cub?" said Kaa.

"Now where do you suppose he could be," continued Shere Khan.

"Search me," replied Kaa.

"An excellent idea, Kaa," said Shere Khan. "Show me your coils."

Kaa swallowed and slowly unwound the outermost coil from Mowgli's body and lowered it slowly down and into the tiger's view.

When Shere Khan found nothing in Kaa's coil he growled low and said, "Hmm, it seems as if you're telling the truth. Well, if you do just happen to see the Man-cub, you *will* inform me first—understand?" warned Shere Khan as he stroked the underside of Kaa's chin with a *very* sharp claw.

Kaa gulped and said, "I get the point. Cross my heart and hope to die."

Shere Khan nodded.

"Good," he said. "Now I must continue my search for that poor, helpless little lad."

Kaa watched Shere Khan leave and shivered. "Oh, who does he think he's fooling?" he said angrily to himself. "Trying to make believe he wants to help that helpless little lad! Oh yesss, that helpless lad." And he licked his fangs and started to coil up toward Mowgli again.

At that moment Mowgli awoke from his trance and angrily pushed Kaa's body off the tree limb.

The long snake unwound around the limb like a spring, bumping and banging his head along the way.

"You told me a lie, Kaa," Mowgli cried. "You said I could trust you!"

Kaa replied angrily, "I guess it's like you said, Man-cub. You can't trust anyone."

But Mowgli hadn't heard. He was already on his way.

Mowgli had gone only a short distance, however, when he found himself in a large clearing just as a light rain began to fall.

He was so tired and discouraged that he walked up to a tree and sat down, hanging his head between his knees.

Just then a gang of scraggly looking vultures flew over him and started to cackle.

Mowgli looked up.

"Go ahead and laugh," he said. "I don't care."

But instead of continuing their teasing, the vultures suddenly swooped down beside him.

"Hey now, kid," said one vulture, named Buzzie. "We were only joking. Why, you look like you haven't got a friend in the world."

"I haven't," sniffed Mowgli.

"Haven't you got a mother or a father?" asked another vulture, named Dizzy.

"No," replied Mowgli. "And nobody wants me around."

"Yeah, we know how you feel," said another, named Flaps.

"Nobody wants *us* around, either," added Dizzy.

"So that's it!" cried Buzzie. "Birds of a feather should stick together!"

"Yeah," said Flaps, "let's all stick together!"

At that moment Shere Khan, who had been crouching near the edge of the clearing, padded forward and applauded.

"A lovely speech," he purred to the vultures. "And thank you for detaining the Man-cub."

When the vultures saw Shere Khan, they scrambled to get away so frantically, their feathers flew in every direction.

"Run, friend, run!" they shouted to Mowgli.

But Mowgli stood his ground.

"Run?" he said. "Why should I run?"

Shere Khan flashed a toothy smile.

"Why should you run?" he purred. "Can it be you don't know who I am?"

"I know you all right," answered Mowgli. "But you don't scare me."

"Ahhh," sighed Shere Khan. "You have spirit. And for that you deserve a sporting chance. I will close my eyes and count to ten. One . . . two . . . three . . ."

When Shere Khan got to ten, he opened his eyes. But instead of running away, Mowgli had picked up a heavy branch and was still facing him.

"You're trying my patience!" he roared. "No more games then!"

And with that, Shere Khan bared his teeth and sprung at Mowgli.

Mowgli was struck with fear as he watched the ferocious tiger come straight at him.

12

*J*ust as Shere Khan was about to pounce on the helpless boy, he suddenly stopped in midair and crashed to the ground.

Mowgli looked behind the tiger in surprise and saw Baloo holding on to Shere Khan's tail!

"Baloo!" cried Mowgli.

"Run, Mowgli, run!" cried Baloo.

"Let go of my tail, you big oaf!" yelled Shere Khan.

But Baloo didn't dare let go.

Then Shere Khan let out an angry roar and spun around and bit Baloo on his backside.

"Yeoow!" yelled Baloo. "That sure didn't tickle!" But he held fast to Shere Khan's tail.

In the meantime, Mowgli had regained his courage and now came at Shere Khan, hitting him on the nose with his branch.

The vultures, who were now safely in a tree, urged him on.

"That's it. Let old Stripes have it, kid," shouted Buzzie.

Shere Khan roared in anger and chased Mowgli around the clearing, dragging Baloo along with him.

"Ouch, oooh, uff!" cried Baloo as he bumped into branches and rocks, still doggedly holding on to Shere Khan's tail.

Mowgli tried to escape, but it was a losing battle. Shere Khan was too fast for him.

"Hey, the kid needs help!" yelled Flaps.

At that, the vultures flew down and picked up Mowgli just as he was about to be bitten by Shere Khan.

"The kid's safe now," Dizzy yelled to Baloo. "You can let go."

"Are you kiddin'?" cried Baloo. "There's teeth on the other end."

Baloo was still trying to figure out what to do when Shere Khan suddenly stopped short and, with a mighty backward spring, flipped the old bear over his head.

In a blinding flash, Shere Khan was upon him.

"I'll kill you for this!" he roared as he started to claw at the helpless Baloo.

Meanwhile, from up in the air Mowgli cried, "Let go! Baloo needs help!"

Suddenly, a bolt of lightning crackled down from the sky and hit a dead tree. With a loud hiss, the tree burst into flames. "That's it!" cried Dizzy. "Fire! That's the only thing old Stripes is afraid of!"

The vultures dropped Mowgli to the ground, and he picked up a burning branch.

"We'll help you!" cried Dizzy as he and the other vultures attacked Shere Khan from the air.

The angry tiger snarled and clawed at them.

"Stay out of this, you mangy fools!" he roared.

But the vultures kept attacking.

This gave Mowgli the chance to get behind Shere Khan and tie the burning branch to his tail.

When Shere Khan looked behind him, he snarled in fright and tried to claw the branch away. But the burning branch stubbornly clung to his tail. And with one last terrified roar, Shere Khan bolted away into the jungle.

Mowgli and the vultures laughed as the big tiger disappeared from sight.

"Old Stripes took off like a flaming comet, he did," cried Dizzy.

"Well, that's over," said Buzzie, looking to

where Baloo was lying on the ground. "Now let's go over and congratulate our friend."

But as Mowgli turned toward Baloo, he could see that the bear was lying too still. He slowly walked over to him. "Baloo, get up," he pleaded. "Please get up."

He took Baloo's head and gently stroked it. But Baloo just lay there, motionless.

13

Bagheera strode into the clearing, and Mowgli looked to him with tears in his eyes.

"What's the matter with Baloo?" he asked.

Bagheera looked at Mowgli with pity.

"You've got to be brave, like Baloo was," he said.

"Was?" cried Mowgli. "You mean he's . . . he's . . ."

"Gone," said Bagheera. "But everyone will remember the brave deed he did this day in the jungle," Bagheera went on. "One name will stand above all others—our friend, Baloo the bear."

Just then Baloo opened his eyes and said, "Did someone mention my name?"

"Baloo, you're alive!" cried Mowgli, throwing his arms around Baloo's neck.

"Why, you, you big fraud," sputtered Bagheera.

But all Mowgli could say was, "Baloo, I'm so happy you're all right!"

"Right as rain," smiled Baloo, shaking the raindrops from his face.

"Good old papa bear," smiled Mowgli.

A short while later, Baloo was carrying Mowgli on his shoulders with Bagheera in tow.

"Hey, Baggy," Baloo cried. "Too bad you missed all the action. You should have seen how I made a sucker out of old Stripes. Me and the kid."

"Yes, sir," he went on. "Nobody is ever gonna come between us . . ."

Baloo was about to finish the sentence when they heard the sound of someone singing in the forest. And suddenly they saw that they were near man-made dwellings.

"What's that?" asked Mowgli.

"Oh, it's the Man-village," answered Bagheera.

"No, I mean *that*," said Mowgli, pointing to a pretty little girl filling up a jug with water from the river. It was she who had been singing.

"Ah, forget about those," answered Baloo.

"They ain't nothing but trouble."

"No, just a minute," replied Mowgli. "I want to take a closer look. I've never seen one before. I'll be right back!" he yelled over his shoulder as he made his way down a path.

"Mowgli!" shouted Baloo.

Bagheera glanced at Baloo with a knowing look in his eyes.

"Wait a minute," he said. "Let him have a better look."

They both watched as Mowgli climbed a tree overlooking the river and looked down. All of a sudden, the branch broke and Mowgli went splashing into the water.

The girl looked surprised at first, but when she saw Mowgli, she put her hand over her mouth and tittered. Mowgli ran to hide in some bushes but finally peeked out and smiled.

"Why, look at that silly grin on his face," said Baloo. "He looks like he's in a trance or somethin'."

Bagheera just nodded his head wisely.

Just then Mowgli emerged from the bushes and approached the girl. She giggled and started to walk toward the Man-village, carrying the jug on her head. But all of a sudden she dropped the jug, and it rolled over to Mowgli.

"Why, of all the nerve," said Baloo. "She did that on purpose!"

Again Bagheera nodded.

Mowgli picked up the jug and went to refill it from the river. Then he carried the jug on his head as the girl had done and started to follow her into the village.

As he got to the gate he turned and looked toward Baloo and Bagheera. He shrugged his shoulders and smiled.

Baloo gestured wildly.

"Mowgli, come back, come back," he yelled.

But Mowgli just kept on grinning and looking back at the girl. Finally, he waved at them and followed the girl into the village.

Baloo shook his head in dismay.

"Aw, he's hooked," he muttered.

Bagheera smiled.

"It was inevitable, Baloo," he said. "The boy can't help himself. It was bound to happen. Mowgli's where he belongs now."

"I guess you're right," said Baloo.

Then he brightened.

"Well, I'm glad *we* still belong in the jungle," he said, "where all you need are the bare necessities."

Bagheera smiled in agreement.

"So what are we waiting for?" asked Baloo. "Let's move it."

Bagheera nodded, and the two friends turned and headed back into the jungle.

But just before they left Mowgli for good, Baloo turned and looked toward the Man-village once more.

He shook his head wistfully.

"Too bad," he said. "That kid would have made one swell bear."